SINGIN MELANCHOLY

(Unveiling the new horizon)

Published By

SINGING AWAY MELANCHOLY

(Unveiling the new horizon)

Compiled and Edited by

Bishaldeep Kakati

EDITOR'S BIO

Bishaldeep Kakati is a person from the legal profession who has completed his Bachelors in Biotechnology and currently pursuing his Masters in Clinical Psychology. He has been serving as the Assistant General Secretary of North East Debaters Association since the last 3 years and is a lifetime member of Assam Sahitya Sabha since 2016. He has also been associated with many NGO's and has worked immensely in various societal events like anti ragging campaigns, flood donation drives etc. In 2017, he was appointed as the Debate and Personality Development Trainer of Maharishi Vidya Mandir School and has conducted many debate and public speaking workshops as the resource person in many schools and colleges of Assam. In 2017, he became the Editor of *Fire The Pyre* (an International Anthology by PWO).

An ardent fan of writing, Bishaldeep has till date written more than 70 articles, 3 travelogues and around 150 poems. His writings have been published in many National and Regional magazines, dailies and weeklies like Frontier Weekly, Radiance, Storizen, The Asian Chronicle, The Goan, The Assam Tribune, The Sentinel, Eclectic NorthEast, Good Times of North East, NorthEast Today, Gplus etc. Apart from that, Bishaldeep has also been a contributing author of more than 10 International Anthologies.

The Editor is also a debater of repute having established his name in both the Debating and Model United Nations Circuit of Assam, as a participant in the yesteryears and as an adjudicator now. As a socio political commentator, he has also taken part in many talk shows in regional news channels voicing out his opinions in pivotal matters affecting the state and the nation.

Apart from writing, debating, public speaking and anchoring, Bishaldeep also has a keen interest in percussions, playing table tennis and cooking delicacies.

He can be reached at-

Email- deep.kakati99@gmail.com

Facebook id - https://www.facebook.com/bishaldeep.kakati/

Instagram- bishal1811

EDITOR'S NOTE

Life on earth is often fragile and uncertain. It's simply like the waves of the ocean that experience highs and lows. The path of our lives is not always smooth and we need to come across many hurdles that test our patience and inner strength. The year 2020 has been a distressing year for the entire globe, as people had to fight with the deadly corona virus pandemic. Many people lost their lives and many had to face the dire consequences of melancholy due to depression, mental issues and the added pressure of being stranded at their homes without being able to socialize. But one thing that has always motivated the generation to fight against all the odds is the 'classical form of art', be it writing, painting, singing etc created by the artists. Therefore, when this pandemic was at its peak, an effort was made by writers across the globe to create something that would provide positivity to the people to see the source of the light coming from far away amidst the darkness.

'Singing away Melancholy' thus is an effort to eliminate all the troubles, sadness, anxiety and grief that has surrounded the ambience of the people at large in the form of writing. Writers, poets from all around the globe have contributed their beautiful writings to not only focus on their views on life but also on how to see the glistening life that would be blessed to one and all once the hardship ends.

In this International Anthology, every effort has been given from the editorial team to make the writings error free. However, if any error happens to occur due to unforeseen issues or printing issues, then the team would be grateful, if those are pointed to us via the mail id- <u>deep.kakati99@gmail.com</u>.

At this outset, I would like to bestow my heartfelt thanks to all the writers from around the globe who have contributed their beautiful writings and made this project a successful one. Special thanks must also be given to Poetry World Organisation that has taken this unique initiative to come out with an anthology that is directly dedicated to the entire civilization, so that they can read the writings, smile and relax amidst the difficult period.

Therefore we hope this anthology carries forward a message of Positivity, Gratitude and Empowerment in each and every reader's mind.

Regards,

Bishaldeep Kakati

(Editor)

CONTENTS

Poetry World Org.

SOMETIMES

Bishaldeep Kakati

Sometimes it makes me sweat.

And then makes me

Shine like a diamond peerless.

Sometimes it makes me bleed,

And drop tears days after days.

When I gather the words

And the amassed emotions,

Sometimes then,

It makes me lose the evaporating love.

Within darkness,

Sometimes it makes me feel the light.

And when I feel the euphoria,

Sometimes then,

It brings forth the storm.

Again sometimes,

It brings the gust,

That breaks,

The dark night's traumatizing lullaby.

When florets blossom,

Sometimes then,

It makes me smell,

The distressing air

Of rotten thoughts.

Then when the sun calls me,

Sometimes it makes me get drowned,

In the flood of betrayal.

THE LULLABY OF THE DARK

Bipasha Saikia

Twinkling stars scatter in the black sheet,

The rhythm of time alluring

them into constellations,

As silvery blue clouds sway in their lap,

Heralding a night, oh-so-magnificent!

The horizon glows as the white

moon looms into view,

Mysterious woods engulfed in a beautiful silence,

Songbirds flock to their nests;

bidding the day adieu,

As lovesick creatures engage in dalliance.

Howling winds sweep over the woods, so eerie,

As birds of ill-omen, let out a screech,

The lonesome traveler, nervous and weary,

To the wispy shadows, he beseeched:

"Spare me, o' the unseen being,"

But his words drowned

in a soul shattering scream.

As the wind murmurs in their soft ears,

Infants cradle to soft lullabies,

Somewhere a deadly howl echoes,

spelling fear and

Transforming blood into ice.

The howling winds brush

the sleeping flowers in the lea,

Jolting them from their deep slumber,

Crickets and moths shrill in glee,

As the spell of the witches produced ember.

The solitary boatman rows in fear,

As nocturnal sounds loom near,

Who let out a whisper in the pale moonlight?

Was it the maiden in white?

Arcane hills, old as centuries,

Shine in the night, like rugged carnivorous jaws.

Monsters of the night join in a chorus,

As the artist gapes in awe!

Ashen clouds cover the orb of the night,

Beloved fireflies descend into oblivion.

Thunder screams across the sky, in might,

And harbingers of death

spread their sharp talons.

Death mist rises from the stream,

Soaking wet, this mysterious night, a beguile,

The glistening of the moonlight,

a song of the dream,

The starlit sky and the moon, a poem of wile.

Who can state:

What this night portend?

A blessing or a bad omen?

SWEET RESPONSE

Mantim Mani Borah

Oh! My glorious feathered friends,

Your splendour does me so enthral,

Through the lonely evening I love to gaze

As on the lake you rise and fall!

After the weariness of the trying day

For the evening I keenly wait;

In your cheerful abandon, watching you play,

My worries, for a moment, I forget!

Your innocent chirping says once again

Life is not yet bereft of joy,

Though not wanting in sorrow or pain,

The world is still ours to enjoy!

MY FINE WINE

Glory Ogunfunmilakin

My fine wine, do you know you send shivers down my
spine?
Your love light me up like
electricity a lot of times.
With you, I can fly up so high without a jet.
It feels like I have known you before we met.
You're a liquor, just one taste and
I am wanting more.
Is it that we are bonded together by God?

Every day, every night, every time,
you never get out of my mind.
Paradise is where I am, whenever I am with you.
Your bright shining smile
can make the oceans dry.
Let my love show,
grow and flow like blood in your veins.
Get obsessed with me;
let me be your everlasting muse.
The hotness between us
can burn us down into flames.

I want to be the bones in your flesh which support
your movements.
Your law of attraction sparks me like lightning.
Hope you are ready to get
drunk in love under my tent?
I don't mind if you eventually
have OD because of me.
Be the fuel in my burning fire of love,
let it double.
To be together forever is what I want with you.

MINDLESS

Saadiya Afzal

Gates shut.
Doors closed.
Locked in a place,
Thinking how to fight at a basic pace.
A battle unknown to the world,
A battle with yourself all alone.
Holding the urge to end it all.
Or calling or messaging the
toxic one that recalled.
Years or months later after they left you bleeding
yourself to fall.
Walls coming closer to squeeze
every ounce of your being.
Mirrors shouting back like a
sword piercing through me.
For the person looks at it
with a throat wrenching sob,
Breaking the soul like a woodcutter cuts his logs.
Voices echoing all around;
Calling names which were never
the ones I was too fond of.
Crushing of soul like never before!
All alone yet with these monstrous thoughts,
Fighting battles of the unknowns.

LIFE ISN'T COMPARABLE

Nandini Mehra

Life isn't easy weather it's a boy's life
Or a girl's life.
Just like some things are not comparable.
Someone is said to wear what they don't want to
And someone is said to be that
what they don't want to be.
Someone is said to cry louder
to show your emotions,
And the other is said to deal it in the quietest way.
Someone is said to stay pleasing and don't argue
Even when she tries to explain her point!
Whereas the other one who might,
Don't want to shout
But say:
Why you stay quite?
Shout it on!
After all you are a man.
Someone is said to don't roam at night
And someone is told to roam out,
"It's your right."
Someone is said to learn cooking
when some wants to fly.
And the other one is told to fly when they want to
achieve their dreams, their wishes.
Some things are not comparable!

Some people are not bad just
because of their gender.

Some emotions are not always expressed!
Someone's life isn't that easy
the way you thought it to be!

WHERE DOES THIS WORLD GO?

Jugesh Singh Thakur

By forgetting the parents affection
And making them cry on every step,
Grieve and sob!
Where does this world go?

By teaching the lessons of life,
And showing false gratitude,
By curving stones and shaping God,
Where does this world go?

By spending hot noon under the shades,
And cutting them unsually,
Setting the world under fire,
Where does this world go?

By shedding tears of birth givers
Leaving them alone, restricted,
And breaking their numbers using words,
Where does this world go?

Night is of every morning, doesn't matter stir
By hailing everyone in heart, showing love,
With all the hardships of time,
Where does this world go?.
Saying worst to others

Same harshness being delivered in turn
By false support, fake comforts,
Where does this world go?

LIFE AS I AM

Madhuri Lad

There are days when I give a
thought on how life is,
And how it must be!
It is some days me waking up
To pass the day out
without giving importance
To my existence.
On days it is the focused me trying out every
sort of way to
come out of the chaos.
It is me as a friend holding up on pain to
stand undefeated by the waves of seas.
It is me running and
sweating the toxic elements
Of the tempted meanness surrounding!
It is me spreading fragrance as I grow towards
the nature.
It is me the ocean of salt , accepting inner self
as my own symbol of love.

It is me that life is about
and it is me that life is for!

JOURNEY OF LIFE

Sheetal

In the journey of life,
We have learned a lot.
With our open arms,
We have accepted the thought.

In the journey of life,
We have travelled far.
Crossing each hurdle,
By wearing sword of smile.

In the journey of life,
We have fought together.
With step by step,
To a mile by mile.

In the journey of life,
We know where we stand.
With our fighting spirit,
We have crossed that land.

In the journey of life,
With our own strength,
Will be lifting each other,
Till the end.

In the journey of life,
Let's do it together,

To show the world,
We won't shatter.

A LUCID DREAM

Dhruv Patel

I've seen it, in my dream,
The far corner of the world.
It's the ocean, so surreal!
Moana herself would have been amazed,
Like that movie of Nolan's
Can't remember how I got here.
But that doesn't seem to matter
Something else has caught my attention.
Unusually large, unusually red,
The setting sun on the horizon
Even larger is it's reflection.
On the cleanest waters of the ocean,
The red sunshine and too many clouds
Some small, some bigger,
But each one shaped like a heart.
Mesmerizing view, all this together,
Felt like it was all designed,
To fulfill a destiny!
Felt like it was about to end
A lifetime of waiting.
I heard a voice, maybe an echo
Somebody called out my name.
Following the sound, I kept searching
A cool breeze passed by and,
I felt someone's hand on my shoulder

Thousand doubts about this reality.
All gone at once but one remains

'I hope it's her, I hope it's her'
Turned around to look and
That's when I wake up,

I told you it's a dream
And dreams tend to get weird
And I don't know if I ever want to be there,
But if I have to
I know exactly who
I want by my side.
"You"!

LIFE: A STRANGE EVENT

Hemlata Ruparam Mali

Life is full of strange facts,
Where her heart survives for her dreams.
Her destiny gets hacked,
And leaving her to struggle with the same.

Life is full of strange situations.
Where sometimes she becomes helpless!
Being just left with frustrations,
And feeling hopeless.

Life is full of strange facts,
Where goals are strived by five,
And yet some forget to appreciate her acts
Though she has helped them in bringing their dream
come live.

Life is full of strange ups and downs,
Learning many experiences,
And some leading to drowns,
Which make her serious now.

TO LIFE

Najam Us Saher

I will smile even when you are giving me a thousand
reasons to cry.
I will be fair with you-my life.
Even though you are so unfair to me.
I will not be the way you had been with me,
Because I want to be remembered as the one
Who smiled in spite all of her grief.
I want to be remembered as the one
Who kept on repeating her mistakes and never failed to
admit them.
I want to be remembered as the one
Who had endless hope and
her expectations ruined her,
You had crushed me and choked me to death,
I am a little distance away from dying,
But you are so cruel,
You take away the lives of others,
who are happy in their lives.
You steal the breath of those
who struggle to be alive,
And don't grant death to those
who don't want to live.
You are a bitter truth,
Now death seems a beautiful lie,
But you are still so cruel to give me hope
That tomorrow will be better.

Since all these years I've lost and been hurt,
You have kept me trapped,
I hate the sunshine and another day,
That couldn't bring brightness in my life.
Each day I am struggling,
Life is sustaining me even
when I don't want to be alive.

ON A PENSIVE NOTE

Shailee Banerjee

Stranded on islands

Fighting lone battles,

Of expectations and reality

Of heart and life!

What u want and what u get?

Confusion and contradictions,

Of the said and the unsaid.

A common bond: Is it there??

Carry on! Fight on!

May be you win,

But

A new battle begins.

Stranded on an island,

We fight lone battles!

THE COUNTDOWN BEGINS

Nahid Belal

The countdown begins
From the moment you were born,
Towards that ultimate fate.
Towards that ultimate death.
You were born to die.
This is the first and last truth
Of your life.
All you have done
From the moment of your birth
And all you will do
Till your last breath
Will take you there
Where we all belong.
Death is that which is
The truth of life
And life is that
We all need to survive.
No matter what you do; right or wrong.
You are just a part
Of that eternal countdown.

MELODY OF MY LIFE

Jyoti Gogia

Staggering reverence in repugnant scenarios.
Life is balancing the acclaim and opprobrium.

Moving on with blisters parched in the feet.
Life edifies to move ahead ruthless ambiguity.

Reminiscing the plethora of scoffing.
Life eulogizes the value of every moment.

A profound coruscate life is worthless.
When a little plight devastates all glee.

In this world of glossy and matte,
I want a life with iridescent generosity.

Conquering all odds and wearing
the tiara of victory.
Life is sometimes worthy of losing good cards.

Stead fastened with a
crashed kaleidoscopic plan-A.
Life finds meaning when we change to plan-B

When failures made me kneel down in despair,
Life unties all the melancholic ties to spare.

Challenges are a part of life and I am a victim,
Yet resuscitating like phoenix and
living dreams is life.

Life is abstrusive and ineffable still euphonic.
Life juxtaposes together both

mystery and magic.

AISLE OF LIFE

Zoya Hassan

I walked down the aisle of life

Claimed to be melancholic.

But was untenanted!

I gaped at my heart

It longed to be filled.

With white blood cells of peace,

Red blood cells of love

And platelets to cover up

Injuries of heartbreak!

I wandered to search these

Woods and open

Without even looking at myself

Then I realized,

It's all enclosed in my mind.

Which needs to disclosed,

To sooth the heart and ultimately my life.

WOMB TO THE TOMB

Monica Mackness

Blossoms of spring

Mighty hills, roller-coaster is the earth's abide.

Blend in to make a new world

Bend down and you shatter your own world

Streams of water as gushes forth

So is every teary eye leaving a mother's womb

Naked body you come to this world

Naked soul is all you carry

when you leave this world.

LIFE

Baisaki Das

I hate myself for being hard,
I'm just a pest who often needs a guard.
I'm weak and I'm not strong
Often you'll see me mourn.

I'm so useless to the world
Go ahead and Pierce the sword.
No one cares about me,
I'm no one's first choice it seems.

I'm neither talented nor beautiful.
I'm so tired of being so "useful"!
Using me to keep you happy,
But you act like a bitch
Whenever I'm happy

I'm just a bug in your life,
Don't even bother giving me a dime
"You're so special," they say.
"I'm not even an essential," I say

LIFE

DANCE IN THE RAIN

Mita Das

It was raining very heavily. Mitul was waiting for her bus at the bus stop, half drenched. She saw a few kids dancing on the opposite side of the road. She smiled seeing them. They seemed happy and carefree, away from worries, dancing with each other happily. Seeing them, she remembered the last time she danced in this carefree manner. She was a kid at that time, just like them. Whenever it rained, she along with other children of her locality would run and dance in the rain, happily singing and dancing, making paper boats and getting dirty in the mud.

She was thinking about her childhood days, when the bus came and stopped in front of her. She came back to the present seeing the bus. A few people hurriedly entered inside the bus, she stood still for sometime. She saw the bus then she saw the happy children. She kept seeing them very quietly. The bus left, taking the passengers, but she remained standing.

She closed the umbrella. It was raining very heavily so she started to get wet but she cared least about that, she crossed the road smiling and stood in front of the kids. The kids stopped dancing when she suddenly appeared in front of them. Then she opened her arms and joined them. The kids again started to dance. She danced like them, happy carefree, avoiding all the strange stares. People thought she must have gone mad, some thought how shameless she was, who was dancing in front of everyone, fully drenched. But she least cared about them.

Life is not always about working according to the expectations of the people and the society. There is a kid hidden in everyone's hearts, but somehow we forget it. Life is not always about pleasing others, and acting according to the rules set by the society. Sometimes we need to be carefree; we need to bring out that kid.

LIFE THROUGH A PEEP BOX

Nupur Pal

I saw children running along the street
As the peep show man drew near,
Oh! What joy glistened in their eyes,
And it was as if they started to
forget all their fear.
Tempted, I also passed through my door,
Soon to be surrounded by an excited crowd,
Since I too wanted to be happy
And wanted to lose myself into
the life beneath that shroud.
As I looked through the glass
I found a whole new world inside,
With blue waters of undisturbed shining rivers,
And those lush greenery by which
I can never bide.
I found unvisited monuments
So high and proud did they stand,
Surrounded by people of different nations,
Some coloured and some bland.
Oh! what joy did I feel
As I explored life through a glassy hole,
But as I moved away from it,
The colour changed into a realistic dull whole.

WORLD REVOLUTION

Mem Milen Snaitang

When the whole world is in doom,
fam'lies united at home,
From the Brahmins to the Harijans,
Politicians to the barbarians;
for some...isolation, a depression;
Well I say it's a mind evolution!
We live only once, someday we'll all die,
Still for the poor child, we turn a blind eye;
The white discriminating the black,
Even now in the midst of this plaque.
The same air we're breathing,
Then why so much boasting?
For peace you cannot buy,
And money can't rely.
Hence this speaks volumes:
We're in the same room.
We've been through the division,
yet through this revolution,
If you would have understood
the beautiful collision;
There's much more than Marxism,
We need more moralism;
No country is alien,
We are made to be one.

JUST ANOTHER 'LIFE STORY'

Vaishnavi Chori

Life's a blank sheet waiting to be coloured,
By the experiences flooded in our conscience,
A blank reminder of all the dreaded failures,
A foundation for building
endeavours of tomorrow,
The canvas of life can be painted by choice-
Negatives or positives
depend on the rationale of our minds.
Life is a never ending
symphony of playful thoughts,
A ballad of untold, unexpressed,
unrequited love stories,
A witness to deprived, depressed, denied times,
A melancholy of stringed remembrances,
A tale of withering and fading opportunities,
A heap full of grief-stricken incomplete stories,
An epitaph of lost people,
who fortunately faked concern,
A swansong of achievements and fulfilments,
An affirmation of optimistic,
joyful tryst with destiny,
A burial place for guilty regrets,

an incessant journey,
A signed treaty seeking expiration
in hour of death,
Life isn't just a story, it's poetry in free-verse.

THE CAUSE

Shona D' Souza

Saddened by the cause,

The cause that gathers a grawl,

Grawling through and through,

Through the dark clear woods.

Growling, screaming, brawling,

To make it turn, make it wither,

Change the cause or change it all,

I don't like it, neither does anyone,

It's a hell of a blur,

Hurting you until it's done,

Why o why doesn't it go?

Change it's course or just find another?

Hate to know that it's still gonna show,

Not gonna wither and maybe just gonna flow.

ALIVE

Pranjalika Sabat

Destined like mirage.
Surprised like firefly in sunshine.
Happiness like once in a blue moon.
Curious like mongoose climbing heights.
Span, same as that of sparrows chirping around,
Unaware of short lived joy.
This is what makes me feel alive.
Venomous taunts of orthodox around,
Could've been my chains but it got rusted.
For my path is blessed with almighty's grace,
Flames of robustness evolved thrashing those bizarre
winds of criticism.
Wielded enough to break bounds.
Shielded like new crockery.
Folded acts of Juvenescence haunting once in a while,
tickling rarely.
Rhyming a soliloquy in the stage of life.
As an Odysseus to my approaching days, often
wondering here & there.
This is what makes me feel alive.

WHEN I WROTE MY OWN

BIOGRAPHY

Ruby Rajesh Yadav

Our whole life we lived making our future bright but we never doubted that isn't our present life so dark just because we always lived in the past and made things for the future?

There are no rules in life until you make some for yourself and life is different just as we want but not exactly with the people we think.

All these years we lived life king size till then we realized we weren't the king since we worked like slaves for almost half of our lives and at last, when a new disease hugs us, we actually shake hands with reality. We meet the reality and are left with nothing that we always ran for because no amount of money is going to cure you and no doctor is god.

It's easy for us to praise people when they worship success but it's not the same in case of the ones who just failed and moved ahead in life because eventually they failed to be what society expected them to be and now their efforts are wasted.

We always took our hair for granted until it started speaking colors since we fooled around from making them black with dyes to white for our kids and silver for our grandkids and never made it gold for ourselves because old is gold. We built houses for our own shelter but when we grow old we realize that we had our kids living with us too so why not get them to knowledge about the house they lived in and are living in. That's what gets us back and we win that too but in the wrong way. We again put all our efforts to someone who is somebody to us, we always give value to the ones who are going to return us the same value we invest in, we move on without appreciating ourselves and again we lose for ourselves and let others think that we are the winners who never painted failures in the art of life.

We would pass all the pats to the ones who are important in our life and never got ourselves praised!

I got myself some lessons to learn at a ripe age but we all know that sometimes life got different plans for us. I wondered how people got success on the front page of newspapers and later vanished like they never existed. I always wanted the success mantra but successful people mislead me saying that there's no elevator to success. Maybe I was living a false life till then success met me on the path towards love, the path I choose. We have always been jailed in our thoughts for being a culprit who kidnapped ourselves and murdered our dreams just because someone called 'society' would never accept us. But when we have completely gone wrong and made things worse for ourselves we realize that it's not easy being us.

I always wanted to be someone I was born to be and I did be but maybe by living someone else's dream, and I promised myself each time I failed that no matter what one day I will become my own hope and here I'm the girl who always made less friends and sat at the cornered last bench, the girl who never scored well and failed to achieve dreams she was made to dream. But now that I am a people's person

I made myself so successful.

I wrote more but my pen cried no more tears and I finally realised that to write down your feelings you need a good pen. Love, money, and people vanish and you are only left with you, who has never tasted praise and loses hopes for living life, you give up on yourself and again life wins, you lose.

Life is a teacher forever and we are the learners who are just bothered by our success and failure.

In the end I would say "Fall in love for success but don't forget to adore yourself and praise your efforts even if you fail because we remember our failures more than our success!"

And everyone in the audience started clapping at the drop of a head, I just got so happy but then I could hear Mom saying something while she was sitting on the front seat and rubbing my eyes I got up to know that I was sleeping and it was all a dream, all the interview and me saying things in front of a huge audience. Everything seemed to be too real to dream of and I got the award of best selling writer for which in reality

I wrote no book. But that was the first time I dreamt the truth that never lied to me, I never dreamt of being someone I just wanted to be. I could be a good writer to write my own biography but it's easy to praise yourself and hard to write good things about you.

BLISSFUL LIFE

Rufeeya Tarannum

Sometimes bumpy, sometimes smooth,

It is always full of youth.

Sometimes dull, sometimes exuberant,

Yet makes every moment vibrant.

Sometimes you smile, sometimes weep,

Every lesson it teaches is deep.

Sometimes disappoint, sometimes amuse,

Gives a feeling you cannot refuse.

Its journey is shaped by paths you take,

Upshot comes from the decisions you make.

So never sulk, never complaint,

To its traits, make yourself acquaint.

Accept life the way it is,

You will realise life is a bliss!

MISSED MOMENTS

Heena Arif

When I was a little child,
My life was filled with so much joy.
Then on seeing those youngsters,
I just wanted to grow up faster.

That college group I used to see,
To me they seemed so happy.
No boring uniforms to wear,
Dress how you like and just cheer.

But then, when I joined college,
Found out it wasn't a happy voyage.
I felt as if I missed something,
Whenever I saw people working.

It made me want to strive so hard,
And get a job for a life unscarred.
I did get a well paid job,
But seeing the couples made me sob.

I got married to my soul mate,
But still I felt so incomplete,
Joy is in enjoying your present life,
It took so long for me to realize!

LIFE IS A GAME

Renu Mangtani

Life is a gamble,
So you better play your turn,
So what if destiny is uncertain and stern,
Thoughts in mind, and never be down,
There is nothing to complain and blame,
Life is just a game,
So, keep that smile on your face,
And, you will win through the race,
Life is a gamble, so play your game,
Go ahead and make your name!
When you will win some and lose some
Are you prepared to face the race
That too with a loving grace
Are you prepared to smile all through
With all the difficulties and trough
Think of something before its late
It is all there in your fate
You just have to think for it!
So Keep Learning Keep Shining!
This is what Life is all about!!

PERFECT

Subhashish

Niche for Souls!

Beyond the cacophony of reality.

Be the part of musical Dreams

Dreams may seem to be inoculated

With abstractions and falsehoods!

Let not our eyes and senses

Be the arbitrators of Doomsday

Our spirits may seem to be neophytes

However, only ones capable of inferring!

Abdicate yourself to nature and nothingness

Be the part of an absolute niche for souls

Niche may seem to be bizarre spot

But, each wandered soul has to stay with may!

Alas! Whither do we waste time instead of searching

the truth

That disappoints and kills souls

in the perfect niche!

THE LABYRINTH

Arthur Ephy Yunan

Sometimes the unspoken truth returns
Sometimes it attacks it's owner viciously
Sometimes it revels in chaos and becomes a lie
Freedom blooms in saying the unsaid
Violence of the bad relies on
the silence of the good

Vision has blinded those it masters
Life has killed those it rules
Medicine has poisoned those it mastered
Sometimes enough is all we need
Too much and it becomes dangerous

Followers of the path have often fallen
Strayers from the path have often risen
The destination has often
found non Walker's of the path
Destiny is a thoroughly twisted endeavor
A game to be played by the powers that be

I have seen powerful men crumble to ashes
I have seen the weak men rise to glory
I have seen people that never desire in more
It's all a game and we are all pieces
Only the player sees the entire picture

LETTER TO MY LIFE

Ananya Panigrahi

Dear Life,

I know you are not about a bed of roses but you are a bundle full of experiences and struggles that I go through every day. You promised me a lot but what you have given me has overshadowed all that you promised. I know that both beauty and beast would come my way, for nothing comes easily in life. You have enclosed both good and bad, because you have made me understand very well that nothing comes undiluted.

When I consider the present, I realise that the happiness of life is in   all these experiences . When I try to achieve my dreams, you pull me down. You teach me the value of patience. You teach me that life is like a flowing river. You make me flow over and around difficulties. I choose for myself now in different times on account of the lessons you have taught me. By choosing not to identify myself completely with difficulties that came my way, I look beyond them and myself despite my multiple identities to the spiritually awakened self that lies inside me.

So when I feel, you are out of my control and that you are way too stressed out to function- I just take a second to step back and breathe. Rome wasn't built in a day, and it is far from perfect. Remember that on your journey, nothing will ever be perfect and it never has to be. There will be times when you will be broken, there will be times when you will feel lonely and sad, but there will be times you will be happy. You'll find that you love all your imperfections and that's the beauty of it! There will be good and bad, but I promise the good will always take over the bad. Just take things one at a time and remember to breathe.

You know, I am still learning and developing myself through my journey. Can you do me a favour? Can you make some of my wishes come true?? Can you fulfill my wishes like a Shooting Star?

Yours,
Someone with dreamy eyes.

THINKING THOUGHTS

Ayushi Singh

Day by day year after year,
Meaning of life is still not clear.
Successful life or the happy soul
Nothing is properly defined at all.
Present, future or past!
All teaches us an important part.
From the morning to the night
Each day adds something valuable in our life.
From loving to breaking,
From teaching to healing!
These to and fro motion of
happiness and sorrow
Live them at that moment
Because in life
There's no full stop.
In the world full of human,
Where humanity has died!
Spreading love and sharing smiles
These are not just thoughts but
the goals of my life.

REMEMBER: YOU WERE BORN TO LIVE!

Jasmine Parveen

Whenever you feel so down,
Don't forget your invisible hair crown.
This world is so hostile,
Always remember, you are versatile.
Always remember to shine and be positive, remember,
you were born to live!

Wake up from cemetery,
Collect your tears and make your military.
Time in a watch never stops,
When life will fly, we never know
No matter how ugly your life,
Remember, you were born to survive.

People may cut your heart in pieces,
But always try to spread the peace.
You may fail thousands of times,
Don't worry,
God sees all your efforts.
You just keep trying,
Your fate is already written.
So, don't be upset or lose your heart,
Remember, you were born to be brave

ESSENCE OF LIFE

Khansa Fatima

You trembled my existence,
My longings were falling apart,
You crushed my desires,
My intimate shadow was ready to depart.

You confiscated my psyche,
My heart was lifelessly cold,
You drained my worth,
My ardour is still bold.

You stretched my twinge,
My faith was dormant,
You inflicted the nuisance,
My wit was in torment.

You shattered the I,
My backbone is imperishable,
You mend the I,
My quintessence is cherishable,

Oh thee my life,
Sculpted me so wise,
Oh thee my life,
Made me a Phoenix who would rise.

A CRAZY LONG DRIVE

Dhanya Ravi

Life is not always a smooth journey drift
For that might drive you right and left.
Start your journey with full of determination
To show that you can
reach up to your destination.

The life journey will happen only once,
So for a long drive, avoid carrying sorrow of tons.
The journey can give you
experiences sweet or bitter
But if you decide to make things better.

Then drive on the right way and
turn out the odds
Also be brave to face all the rough roads.
Stay strong to decide on tough trips
But make sure to avoid harsh ones that strips.

Be confident, look forward and drive
ahead with your head up.
Even when you drive into
a valley deep or a hill up,
Don't stop your journey in the mid way
For later on drive, regrets to say.

Make love with each moment of your life journey
To enjoy the drive with bliss and harmony.
Life is not always a smooth journey drift
But only you can make the drive
a memorable gift.

my man

Alisha Khanam

Ohh! Look at the little one,
His smile is beaming like the sun.
His vibes, His smile,
His shiny eyes are coherent
Gushing and rushing like a torrent.

The toddler boy
Now a teenager, gleams with a smile
Ah! He's coy!
Feelings, emotions,
confusions and complications
All made home in his heart.
He ignores but sometimes it hurts,
But he didn't let it tore him apart.

The man in him now
Speaks with confidence.
The pain made him strong
It's not a coincidence.
Once a falling star, now someone's moon
Lightning up her dark world.
He holds her hand tight
No more she swoons.

Fortuitously, we're together
Oh beloved! I wish it lasts forever.
Blessings and wishes from my heart.

May our love be like the cosmic rays.
We stay together forever like rose and scent
May God bless us and never
keep our hearts apart.

WHAT IF?

Ian Otieno

Sometimes I sit by the riverside to
listen to noisy songs,
Fingers to support my chin as I smell the sweet acrid
air like a doll,
Eyes to the looming orange evening sky ball,
To the visible gradient of blue on
the eastern side sky goal,
Stars eager to make the
night's performance in bold.

Staring deep, my eyes ask
the oblivious sky of blue,
What if life was fair and everyone was stinking rich
without school?
What if there was no struggle and
success fed by a spoon?
What if intelligence wasn't viewed by performance
inside the classroom?
What if judging was made a crime by the constitution
of doom?

What if time was visually predictable and the future
was defined?
The past a gateway to the
future that never passed?
The present to never matter and

degrade to the past?
What if time travel was possible in just a blast?
What if the nature of reality was unleashed?

What if the fabric of the cosmos got torn?
The spectacle of the universe wore
spectacles when born?
The string theory would come true and get
acknowledgment for long?
What if love was real and would live happily ever after
as in the songs?
Lovers to be loyal and tie not a knot
of lies later to divorce.

TRANSPIRED SPACE

Samparna Dalbehera

She was broken then mended

With slushy emotions and self-love,

Unruffled all the shattered pieces

Astray in the melancholy grove.

Little did she knew

Behemoth roaming all around,

Still she was not petrified

Ceasing all the ardour shroud and bound.

Thinking of tranquil

Searching for solace to hide in,

She didn't forgot self-love

Kept silence and fervour packed within.

She was alike an alternating current

Fluctuating like switching events,

Dwelling and drooling in her own space

Relishing the sapid moments.

Once she transpired out of her space

Felt free and budged with grace,

She had a thought on her mind

Why she was un-clued of this place?

SILENCE: MY SAD QUIETNESS

Khushi Jariwala

I am here,

Somewhere,

I am in deep silence,

I cry a lot but it's quiet!

I love a lot but it's calm!

It's life! Where I served my sad pie!

Stuff in it is of pain

And tears of pound!

But it's always about me

And my soul!

I got a perfect vow!

To talking whispering slow!

I can't afford being whole!

I am better as I am growing half alone!

Nobody other than silence!

I can't now keep alliance!

That's what my poem shows!

It's all about my quietness vows

RAINBOW AFTER YEARS

Rashmika

They say life is a journey.

Forks in the road

Guided by the hearts of others,

Brushing up against our sleeves.

Yet we will keep on walking!

Dipped valleys for fray skies

A world above out of arms reach,

As the ground swallows us whole,

Yet we still keep on walking!

Climbing the hills

Just to catch a glimpse,

Of the mountains peak.

You may bruise.

You may even break.

Yet we still keep walking.

Because no one said this trip would be easy.

JOURNEY TOWARDS PEACE

Radneswary Sooriyakumar

Amidst the countless commotions

Desired his heart for tranquility!

Little did he know that

Calmness doesn't come with

Inner Turbulence.

Why? why was his heart not in peace?

Where was the peace he longed for

What would give harmony to his heart?

Who can ever aid him in this process?

Brooding with unanswered questions

Deprived his heart of happiness.

On his journey he came across so many

But they were just explanations.

All these explanations mapped him

His answer - The answer which he searched for; has
travelled with him

All along his journey - To look within.

Yeah, the path to peace

Answer to his internal traumas;

Not only his but the harmony of many

Outright of peace and Harmony,

Was Him–Himself!

LIFE

Cornelius Kipkosgei

Life is a souvenir of suicidal mirth,

My neck has been saved many times,

From a gracious noose of a tight rope,

My hands have tormenting scars,

Cut deeply by sharp blades,

My head has seen the realm of the dead,

In visions and flashes that died prematurely,

Beneath this old garb lies wounds,

Wounds that paint a grim picture of memories,

My bright eyes disguise teardrops,

Teardrops that scale my pillow at night,

I have contemplated ending this life,

On second thoughts, I have had a reason to live

If I don't offer second chances, who will?

THE SECOND CHANCE

Ajay Jayavarapu

I was sleeping beside the window gazing at the stars in the half visible sky from my room. One of my ears was filled with music from the earphones and the other ear was filled with a delicate sound of dripping rain drops. My fingers were busy in scrolling all over the social media and my mind was busy in running all over the thoughts that made me feel alone. Even I was unable to realise the song was changed. The music was just running in my ears and it was unable to reach my mind. I know, I'm not asleep but I felt like my mind was pretending to be dead or lying dumb. I know it's the most dangerous time to think about someone but we can't control our thoughts. At these times the feeling emerged out of those thoughts can control us.

It can make you assure that this is going to be another sleepless and lonely night. It can make you feel like everything will be changed by the time you woke up. It can make you believe that you still have a chance. Yes I'm thinking about a chance, actually a SECOND CHANCE. I know I was not ready to go back but at the same time I don't know what's making me think about that. Every second of my loneliness was addicted to the thoughts of that second chance. I know how I struggled and how I fought myself for not to reach these thoughts. But here I'm thinking about the process of how I reached to these thoughts. It made me feel like I can't survive alone. But the thing that you don't know was, I actually used that second chance and failed at it. At the failure of that second chance I still never gave up, instead I waited for another chance.

I never felt insult about my own result. I wondered how I can be sure that this does not work for me. You know what's the beauty of a second chance?? You can have thousands of them. But it depends on how you used it the last time you got a chance. It depends on what changed you and what you changed when you got that chance. CHANCE and CHANGE look like similar words. Even those words were separated by their meanings they need each other. Yes, every chance needs a change and every change needs a chance. When I got a chance I tried to change, but when I changed, I'm still thinking about another chance. Then what should I feel?

"Is it a waste of a chance I took?" or "is it a waste of the change I did?". Still I know I'm not going back but what are these thoughts about? Have you ever questioned yourself like this? Have you ever struggled for answering yourself? I know some of you experienced these but did you got any answers? Sometimes I wanted to ask everyone that "how many times did you tried? Did you keep any count of that?" But I know who can keep a count of how many times they tried. The only answer I can give myself was "I never gave up". But I never thought I'll remain alone with that answer. Some questions made me answer myself and some answers made me question myself. I know I never started with these questions but I ended up answering myself for these questions. Every time I thought about a second chance I questioned myself because it's never easy going back when you decided something. But I did it. I know the value of a second chance because I ruined it the last time. Every time when I ruined it, it ruined me back until I got another chance. I know this is not going to work when I go back, because I know I'll end up thinking about another chance. I never tried to change the meaning of second chance when I got it, because I know that someday the last chance comes in the form of that second chance. No one warned me that it will be my last chance.

I did some things like I did last time when I got a chance. I thought I can get another one by ruining this again. I felt like every chance I got is a last chance and tried to end these thoughts. I made a choice to let it go in the worst possible way because letting it go is never a better way. Finally it was me who let it go, but something inside me is still saying that I never gave up on any chance I got. Still, I got enough courage to buy that chance but I felt like I'm not rich enough to buy that chance anymore. I can move forward by forgetting these thoughts, but I can't forget these thoughts without forgiving myself. I can convince myself. This is not about the chance I got, but this is about the chance I took. I realised that I can't take away some things from me ever again. I can't control me anymore but I still had that power over me. I felt like I can't change anymore but I can like myself for what I am. I used to hurt myself in countless ways, in ways I promised myself that I never would. I used to say I was not afraid of being hurt but now I was afraid of getting used to this hurt. I can still remember the pain of every word that I told myself for getting a second chance. I was told that time heals all wounds. Then what about the lost chances? I guess the time can't do anything about the lost ones. I'm the one who planted this seed and watered with every chance I got. But I never thought these roots will weak the ground I stood by leaving me with no chance. I know that I can't stop these things, so I felt it's better to be ended.

THE LIFE

Monika Shanmugam

Life is a Maya! Life is a mystical Maya!

In which we all born with the

congenital cataract of mind,

That had practiced to see and believe,

The cloudy allures and the hefty illusions,

Camouflaged the lasting truthfulness and the core of
every life's purpose.

O! How long this callow mind survives!

Within its own defect of cataract,

How long!

O Lord! May we acquire wisdom to

treat our mind's opacity,

And get the clear insight of everything in LIFE!

GROWING UP UNDER TARO UMBRELLA

Shabnam Jannat

"Waiting for the train?"

My chain of thoughts was broken by this unknown voice. I looked to my side to find a lady of about the age of forty sitting next to me. She was smiling at me but her eyes, behind those horn-rimmed glasses showed sincere concern. I wondered if I know her but I failed to remember that unrecognizable face. I could not pay attention to what she was asking me so she asked again.

"Are you waiting for the train?"

I didn't have the answer to that simple question. Sure, I was waiting for the train but not for the popular purpose. I was skeptical if this lady understood why I was there. I could not decide if I should reply to her or not. I didn't even know whether she was a stranger or a forgotten acquaintance.

"Hello? Aren't you waiting for the train?"

She spoke to me again.

"Yeah, maybe...if it can kill me."

I responded.

"Oh, okay!"

She did not look surprised at all. She just smiled at me and started reading one of the books from her bag. I wasn't hoping for such an unemotional reaction. And what was that smile for?

"I'm sorry but aren't you even a little surprised?"

"No. I am not at all surprised."

"Why not? Is it a big crime to show a little care for a fellow human being?"

"It is not. But as a matter of fact, I very well know that you are not going to do what you are saying."

"What? Why won't I? That is all I'm here for."

She showcased her annoying smile again and did not say anything this time.

"Are you trying to say that I'm some kind of attention-seeker?"

"Is that what you're sa-a-ying?"

I broke down as I struggled to finish my sentence. I didn't understand why her thoughts instigated me to have a meltdown. It shouldn't matter to me. But, perhaps, deep down I wanted to have a last meaningful talk with someone. For the last time, I wanted somebody to hear me out. Perhaps, that's a lot to ask. And it isn't worth crying for after all that's wrong with my life.

Just as I was lost in my thoughts and tears, I felt the warmth of a hand wrapped around my shoulder. It was the lady. She wiped off my tears and looked at me with stern yet tender eyes.

"What's your name?," she asked me.

"Maya"

"Look, Maya, I did not think that you are, in any way, trying to take this step for attention. It's just that I was in a similar position once. And yet, here I am sitting right next to you with my head held up high. Am I not?"

"I don't think you understand my situation. I have nothing to change my mind for. Moreover, no one would even notice if I disappear. My parents are too busy to care about what I want. They never have time for me. They keep bickering with each other all the time without thinking twice about how I feel. Still, I made my peace with it. But my world collapsed when the only person who actually cared about me and loved me unconditionally, my grandmother, left me last year. Life has only gotten worse after that. My parents sent me off to this new unknown place without my consent. Every person I met in this big city is selfish and dishonest. I have no friends in my new college and all my friends from Guwahati seem to have just forgotten about me. I even tried to make friends here but when I did, I was body-shamed for the way I look. One of them even tried to sexually har-a-ass m-me."

I started sobbing again, this time louder than before. But for some reason, I continued to tell her everything.

"Nothing intrigues me anymore. I have lost all interest in my studies. I am all alone and I have no one to even talk to. All I do is lie down on my bed all day, staring at the ceiling, numb and frozen, tired of breathing, tired of dreaming the same dreams in my sleep."

I couldn't look at her. My vision was blurred by my own sweats of eyes.

"Oh dear!"

She said these words and in a swift move, held me close to her heart. I buried myself in her arms and cried my heart out.

"I can completely understand you. Life is difficult. But that doesn't mean you give up on it. You have to find a reason to live even if it shows you the toughest of times. Everyone has a purpose and when one finds it, life is worth living, my dear. You remind me a lot about myself. I, too, was in a depressed state after I lost my parents when I was ten. My relatives were not very good to me. After all, I was a burden on them. They tortured me every single day. Some days, I did not even get food. So one day, I ran away from home. But I had no where to go. I cried endlessly and finally decided to jump off in the village pond. But as I reached the pond shoreline, a Taro leaf caught my eyes. I remembered how I used to play with these leaves when my parents were alive. How my father and I would use this leaf as an umbrella and walk around in the rain. How my mother would prepare delicacies out of this leaf. And that day, as I was going to end my life, those same leaves were there for me. That is when I realised, I wasn't alone. I grew up with these leaves. It was as if my dead parents were sending their love to me through these leaves and they helped me live. And today, I am sure you will find your Taro umbrella, too. Just give time some time."

And just then, the train arrived and the lady bid adieu to me. It was my chance to put an end to my miserable life. But the lady's words kept running in my mind. What if I find my own purpose if I give life some more time? I suddenly had the urge to fix my life. And with that, I took a step back. I went back home and called my parents. I blurted out everything that was inside of me and hung up the call. The next day was better than usual. I joined a painting class and made a new friend there. I always loved painting and showing them to my grandmother. But after her death, I stopped painting, entirely. It was a mistake. I should have instead kept my grandmother alive with my paintings.

And that's my purpose now.

Going back home, I visited a library where I found the same book that lady was reading the previous night. I read the title and smiled- "Growing up under Taro Umbrella". And just as I figured, the book was written by that same lady. There was a picture of her at the back of the book. But I was shocked as I read what was written below that picture - "Tarali Hazarika (1960- 2001)". I couldn't believe what I was reading. The book says she is dead.

I was shaken to my core.

Was she a ghost? No, she was an angel. She was the star who lit up my starless and somber sky. She was my Taro umbrella who saved my life. And who knows the value of life better than a dead person.

A GIRL

Prerna Malik

In her gleaming eyes resided the perpetual terror of losing her congruence that never came with manual to instruct those who did not know the significance of her life. Her eyes always had the fear of the fake masculinity having the defeated sight of view for they never saw her as a daughter or a sister but something to be sadistically usurped.

Never knew dad could not help her but put her deeper into the jive for her tender arms couldn't bear the height to come out and raise her voice.

Mom saw her crying, blood shredded through her clothes but couldn't dare to choose her daughter over the society and the custom followed again. Her mouth was shut with the hands of agitation and eyes gaped to never utter anything for the sake of her prestige and the family to have a shield over the head. She took her under her stole and made her mum forever.

Turned 16, the ritual still continued, she was getting buried under the disaster and the wounds were still green. She was tired of keeping herself mum and stroked to go beyond the bars to put them behind the bars. She knew people would accuse actions on her soul that never even breathed over the last 16 years.

She relived those horrifying years, saw those pitiless faces again, cried over the punctures again but with a heavy heart she vomited her heart out. They giggled and her arm was grabbed again with ruthless intuitions.

She pushed them back perhaps she lost the ability to raise her voice and could never.

Why was her hand not held for the prevention but for doing the sins?

REALITY

Kiran Chetry

Life is a journey.
We are actor and actress and
almighty is the erector,
Earth is our home not the bungalows,
Our wealth is that supreme god is our father,
Corpus is our cloth not life,
Every people is our family,
We may say we are nuclear family,
But we are join family.
The journey of our cloth is amazing,
Just we have to feel the journey,
Changing clothes in a definite period is extraordinary
feeling.
Good karma is our food,
But every day we are eating stale
food from five vices,
Lust, greed, anger, attachment, ego is your enemy not
friends.
Be aware life is not a game it is a
journey to know yourself.

IT'S YOUR LIFE

Mobani Biswas

My life is unique, so is yours
It's a bouquet of various flowers
including the thorns.
It cannot be categorised as tragedy or comedy
It's a potent concoction of it all.
Don't let others determine the story of your life
Whether a smooth road or a learning curve,
it's for you to decide.
No one would understand your brain and
heart as you do
Take charge of your life and even in darkness, find
your way through.

You being the writer of your own story
Why let others hold the pen for you.
Have the courage to learn from your mistakes
Course you consider apt is what you should take.

The desire to please everyone is
something we should banish
More the people, more the
opinions would flourish.
Some people will always aim to pull you down
Your determination to persevere will be your shining
crown.

LIFE'S LESSONS

Afrose Fathima

I was just brought up as a tiny little kitten.
With no pain of even my tongue has been bitten
Laughter filled my breaths without any adjourn
And nights spent so beautiful
with mom's lovely nocturne.

By then, life met with a tragic turn
And everything changed leaving
no way back to return.
Life turned out dark with
not even a single lantern.

Deep down there in loneliness, with no
one left back to yearn
Just regretted of the lesson... Life has ever given...

Dumped out of betrayal...
Life made my unlearn lessons... learn

People would just wait for their turn
like the bewitched erne.
So man! Seeks no man for concern
Nothing which happened can be rewritten.
The bygone days are never going to return
Not just money in this world we do want to earn.

So travel so long to places like Britain
Taste everything from sweet corn to sauterne.
And enjoy your life as no one has ever written!

I DIDN'T KILL MYSELF

Unnati Kotecha

Just a minute ago I was standing on the edge of my terrace. I could feel the scorching sun under my bare feet. Must have been a hot summer day! The last time I went out it was spring, flowers blooming everywhere. Had I actually lost so much time in my den of 10 by 10? Must be because of the pills. My head aches so bad and so does my wrist. Why does it have so many half healed cut marks? Who did this to me?

Must be Sumer!

He hates me. He said I am sick and not worth his love but why would he say that while he was the one who loved the way my lips tasted after wine. It's all because of her, I know. None other than Kriti I had seen Sumer crushing her body against the wall with his hands all over her. And that bastard says I am unworthy?!! That whore got what she deserved. She was so fragile and stupid. She thought I wouldn't find out ever, but unfortunately I did. So, one day I served her coffee with my pills (Just a little extra than I usually have).

Revenge is like a sweet fulfilling pain which will hit your guts every time you remember the sin it compelled you to commit, and make you puke your guts out. But people don't call it sweet revenge for no reason because when the sin is being committed it feels like one of those sugar candies which instantly melt as you place it on your tongue, leaving sweetness and feeling content. So, when I sliced her throat slowly with a blade and saw blood oozing out, it felt same. Guess the pills worked, she never woke up again, though my bath tub now stinks of blood. But I don't understand who killed my cat? That must be Sumer!

God! My head hurts. I need to sleep too. As I step down the edge of my roof and look down, I see blood. Lots of blood! The girl is dressed exactly like me and even has my kind of hair. IT'S MEE!! It's meee!! I am dead. But who killed me?

That must be Sumer!

ज़िन्दगी एक जंग है..!

Rajni Sharma

ना जाने ज़िन्दगी का क्या रूप है क्या रंग है

क्या है ये ज़िन्दगी, ये ज़िन्दगी एक जंग है

ख्वाहिशों से घिरे हुए बैठे थे एक छोर पर

तिनके सारे समेट लिए धीरे-धीरे जोड़कर

फिर भी ना जाने क्यूँ, ये ज़िन्दगी बेरंग है

क्या है ये ज़िन्दगी, ये ज़िन्दगी एक जंग है

सागर की गहराई को नापा है क्या किसी ने

किनारे पर हो खड़ा, झाँका है क्या किसी ने

क्या ज़िन्दगी सागर में कोई उठती हुई तरंग है

क्या है ये ज़िन्दगी, ये ज़िन्दगी एक जंग है

बेईमानों को जीत जहाँ, ईमानदार को ठोकर मिले

जवानों को पहचान यहाँ ज़िन्दगी खोकर मिले

ज़िंदा इंसानों में ना, अब जीने की उमंग है

क्या है ये ज़िन्दगी, ये ज़िन्दगी एक जंग है

नकाब ओढ़कर यहाँ हर जुर्म छुपाया जाता है

पत्थर दिल इंसान को हीरा बताया जाता है

मुश्किलों का सामना कर ईमानदार बुलंद है

आज मैं समझी आखिर ये ज़िन्दगी क्यूँ जंग है..!

QUOTES

Durgesh JAYAM kurmi

ज़िन्दगी की हकीकत उड़ चले उस आसमां में जहाँ तारे न थे,

देखे जा रहे उस सागर को जिसके किनारे न थे।

हुए जब मदहोश इस ज़िन्दगी की दौड़ से,

तो फ़िर पहुँचे वहाँ, जहाँ कोई हमारे न थे।

आशंका

Shipra S Gupta

विभा काम निपटा कर जैसे ही बालकनी मे आकर बैठी वैसे ही उसकी नज़र सामने वाले घर के लॉन मे बैठी युवती पर पड़ी "अरे! यह तो मालती है", सहसा उसके मुख से निकला। मालती ने शायद उसे नहीं देखा और वो उठ कर घर के अंदर चली गई।

विभा का मन अतीत के पन्ने पलटने लगा। उन दिनों विभा के पति का तबादला कानपुर हुआ था। मालती मेरे घर के पास रहने वाली सुमन की बेटी है। सुमन मेरी छोटी बहन की सहेली है। बचपन से हमारे घर आयी गयी है

तो दोनों घरों में अच्छी जान-पहचान है।

जब मेरे पति का तबादला कानपुर हुआ तो वो बहुत खुश हुई की हम दोनों एक ही शहर में है। वो मेरे घर अक्सर आ जाती थी फिर हम दोनों आराम से हँसते बतियाते और कब समय बीत जाता पता ही नहीं चलता।

एक दिन उसने बताया की उसकी बेटी की स्नातक की पढाई पूरी हो गई और वो घर वापस आ रही है। सुमन बहुत खुश थी। विभा की बेटी मालती भी उसी की तरह सुंदर और सुशील थी। विभा ने मालती की शादी के लिए लड़का देखना शुरू कर दिया था। एक अच्छे घर में मालती की शादी की बात

पक्की हो गई और सगाई भी हो गई।

अचानक शादी से दो दिन पहले सुमन रोती हुई मेरे पास आई। "देखो ना दीदी, मालती घर छोड़ कर चली गई"।

ऐसे कैसे, क्या हुआ सुमन? फिर सुमन से पता चला की मालती अपने साथ पढ़ने वाले किसी लड़के से प्यार करती थी। उसने सुमन से कहा भी की वो उसी लड़के से शादी करेगी, पर सुमन ने उसका रिश्ता कहीं और पक्का कर दिया। इसी बात पर मालती शादी से दो दिन पहले भाग गई।

और एक हफ्ते बाद वापस भी आ गई। जिस लड़के के साथ भागी थी उसने भी चार, पाँच दिन भोग कर उसे छोड़ दिया।

मालती ने अब चुप रहना शुरू कर दिया जैसे वो अपनी गलती पर अंदर ही अंदर घुल रही थी। दो महीने बाद सुमन उसे अपने साथ अपने ससुराल के गाँव ले गई और वही कहीं

उसकी शादी कर दी।

इधर मेरे पति का भी तबादला आगरा हो गया और

मैं फिर एक नए शहर में आ गई।

आज सालों बाद मालती को देख कर सारी बातें याद करते हुए दोपहर हो गई। शाम को पता नहीं कौन-सा मोह मुझे खींच कर उसके घर के दरवाज़े तक ले गया।

घंटी बजाते ही एक उधेड़ उमर की औरत ने दरवाजा खोला।

नमस्ते करते हुए मैंने मालती के बारे में पूछा। वो हँसते हुए वोली "हमारी बहू है मालती, आइये अंदर आइये"। घर के अंदर आने पर बैठते ही वो पूछ बैठी" आप कैसे जानती हैं मालती को"? मैंने उन्हें बताया की मालती और सुमन मेरी करीबी रही हैं। उनके आवाज़ लगाते ही मालती वहाँ आ गई और जैसे ही उसकी नज़र मुझ पर पड़ी, उसके सफ़ेद पड़ते चेहरे को

मेरी अनुभवी आँखे पहचान गईं।

मुझ से नमस्ते करके मालती काम का बहाना कर वहाँ से चली गई। मैं भी ठगी-सी अपने घर वापस आ गई।

उसका सफ़ेद चेहरा मुझ से जैसे बहुत कुछ कह गया। जैसे वो डर गई हो की मै उसकी ज़िन्दगी का वो काला सच कहीं उसकी

सास को ना बता दूँ।

मन ही मन में निश्चय करके मैंने अपने पति से कह कर उनका तबादला कुछ ही दिनों में दिल्ली करा लिया।

जिस दिन मुझे आगरा से दिल्ली आना था। सामान ट्रक में भरा जाने लगा, तभी मालती के घर से चीखने पुकारने की आवाज़े आने लगी। मैं दौड़ कर उसके घर के अंदर गई तो देखा मालती ने ढेर सारी नींद की गोलियाँ खा ली थी और

इस दुनिया को अलविदा कह गई।

मै भौचक अपनी जगह पर खड़ी रह गई और बहते हुए आँसुओ के बीच इतना ही बुदबुदा पाई "थोड़ा तो इंतज़ार कर लेती मालती, मै तो जा ही रही थी, बस यही आशंका थी कि तुम ऐसा कुछ ना कर जाओ"।

ज़िन्दगी

Kiran Talreja

ज़िन्दगी का खेल अब जंग का मैदान बना है....

अपनों की हार में देखते खुद की जीत है....

लफ़्ज़ों से तहज़ीब हर कोई यहाँ गंवा बैठा है......

तौहीन करने का मानो सबको यहाँ अधिकार मिला है.....

खुदको ऊँचा दिखाने के खातिर हर कोई यहाँ लड़ रहा है....

अपनो को नीचा दिखा कर हर कोई नई रीत चला रहा है.....

ज़िन्दगी का खुदा जानो अब पैसा बना है......

उससे बड़ा ना कोई पैगंबर बचा है....

रिश्ते नाते अब कुछ नहीं एक मात्र दिखावा है.....

जीवन के हर मोड़ पर संघर्ष देखो नया खड़ा है.....

चुनौतियों से भरी हुई ज़िन्दगी सबकी यहाँ......

अपना ना किसी को मानो यहाँ हर कोई पराया है......

रिश्तों के सजदे में ना झुकना ये केवल एक छलावा है.......

ऐतबार ना किसी पे करना यहाँ हर कोई कर रहा तमाशा
है......

उम्मीद रखना इस दुनिया में मानो सबसे बड़ा अब धोखा
है.....

मदद अनजान की कर देना मानो अब कोई गुनाह बना है......

उम्मीद ना किसी से रखना ही एक मात्र समझदारी है.....

स्वार्थी, अहंकारी, फरेबी ही अब यहाँ पर प्राणी है.....

खुद पर बस विश्वास रखना कि यही एक अक्लमंदी है.....

जान लो, समझ लो, मतलबी ये दुनिया सारी है.

Poetry World Org.

9 788194 928843